I0823731

INTRODUCTION

OPEN YOUR HEART

What would you do for love? Love is a beautiful and powerful motivator. It makes us move mountains and give up everything for the happiness of our darlings. But what happens when love is dark and full of shadows? What lurks in the depths of your soul? What secrets do you harbor that should never see the light of day? What would you do for love when all the cards are on the table and your soul is ripe with the potential of loss? Would you risk it all—risk all of yourself—to keep your dear ones close?

Gothic works of fiction are typically defined as European writings with haunting prose that delves into the darkest parts of the human psyche. The genre overlaps with elements of sci-fi and supernatural that helps the author speculate on what a person will do when put into impossibly difficult situations. They ask big questions about where morality intersects with the follies of hubris and the nature of the human heart. Lovers of the genre are at home amongst the gloom and love to answer the call of the void.

Romances in gothic fiction are rife with yearning, deep-seated devotion, mystical creatures, and dark questions about grief, loss, and the darker side of love and longing. Their backdrops are dim yet stunning castles with overgrown rose gardens filled with thorns. Heroines and heroes are often too smart for their own good and drive the story with the strength of their convictions.

Though moody and shadowed by premise, gothic romances have an astounding capacity for hope. Love that blooms in these settings is tender and fierce in equal measure. Lovers will walk through hell (whether literal or metaphoric) and come out the other side a resplendent phoenix. Characters' mettle is tested and their heartstrings tugged, and they either emerge at the other side of their journey stronger for the trials they endured or a broken-hearted husk of who they used to be.

Within these pages you'll find quotes from classic novels, plays, sayings, and poems that illustrate the full spectrum of love that thrives and shines brightest in the darkest hours.

Agnes Hollyhock is a lifelong Wiccan with an affinity for runes casting and tarot reading. She practices her craft in the Northeastern United States, where she lives with her beloved pet companions, cat Jack and tarantula Sally.

ETERN

A devoted heart can transcend life and death. The truest love is the love that lasts beyond the bounds of this mortal coil. When spirits intertwine and hearts touch, there's nothing that can separate them.

AL

LOVE

. . . his indescribable little air of knowing nothing in the world but love.

From *The Turn of the Screw* by Henry James

If he loved with all the powers of his puny being, he couldn't love as much in eighty years as I could in a day.

From *Wuthering Heights* by Emily Brontë

A little while, and all this will appear a dream. I shall look, and cannot see you; shall try to recollect your features—and the impression will be fled from my imagination;—to hear the tones of your voice, and even memory will be silent!—I cannot, cannot leave you! Why should we confide the happiness of our whole lives to the will of people, who have no right to interrupt, and, except in giving you to me, have no power to promote it? . . . Venture to trust your own heart, venture to be mine forever!

From *The Mysteries of Udolpho* by Ann Radcliffe

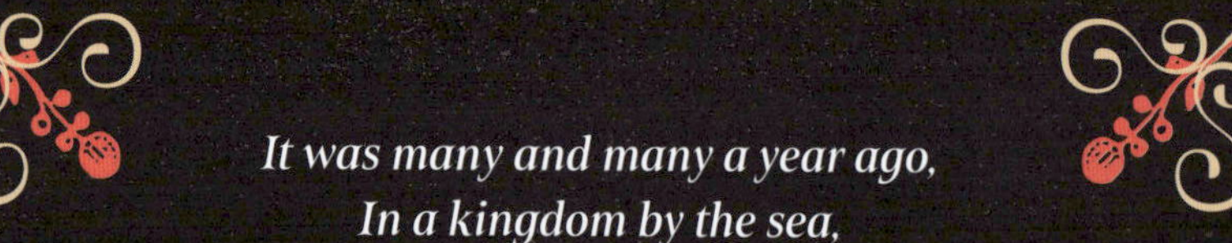

It was many and many a year ago,
In a kingdom by the sea,
That a maiden there lived whom you may know
By the name of ANNABEL LEE;
And this maiden she lived with no other thought
Than to love and be loved by me.

I was a child and she was a child,
In this kingdom by the sea;
But we loved with a love that was more than love,
I and my Annabel Lee;
With a love that the winged seraphs of heaven
Coveted her and me.

. . .

But our love it was stronger by far than the love
Of those who were older than we,
Of many far wiser than we,
And neither the angels in heaven above,
Nor the demons down under the sea,
Can ever dissever my soul from the soul
Of the beautiful Annabel Lee.

For the moon never beams without bringing me dreams
Of the beautiful Annabel Lee;
And the stars never rise but I feel the bright eyes
Of the beautiful Annabel Lee;
And so, all the night-tide, I lie down by the side
Of my darling, my darling, my life and my bride,
In the sepulcher there by the sea,
In her tomb by the sounding sea.

From "Annabel Lee" by Edgar Allan Poe

"Come to me—come to me entirely now," said he; and added, in his deepest tone, speaking in my ear as his cheek was laid on mine, "Make my happiness—I will make yours."

From *Jane Eyre* by Charlotte Brontë

I'll tell you . . . what real love is. It is blind devotion, unquestioning self-humiliation, utter submission, trust and belief against yourself and against the whole world, giving up your whole heart and soul to the smiter—as I did!

From *Great Expectations* by Charles Dickens

Darling, darling. I live in you, and you would die for me. I love you so.

From *Carmilla* by J. Sheridan Le Fanu

For us, for you and for me, there is only one thing that matters, whether we love each other. Other people we need not consider.
Why are we living here apart and not seeing each other? Why can't I go? I love you, and I don't care for anything.

From *Anna Karenina* by Leo Tolstoy

OF ALL
THE HORRORS
WE COULD FACE,
THE WORST WOULD
BE TO FACE THEM
WITHOUT
EACH OTHER

Unknown Author

He knew that when he kissed this girl, and forever wed his unutterable visions to her perishable breath, his mind would never romp again like the mind of God. So he waited, listening for a moment longer to the tuning-fork that had been struck upon a star. Then he kissed her. At his lips' touch she blossomed for him like a flower and the incarnation was complete.

From *The Great Gatsby* by F. Scott Fitzgerald

He pines for kindness, as well as love; and a kind word from you would be his best medicine . . . He dreams of you day and night, and cannot be persuaded that you don't hate him, since you neither write nor call.

From *Wuthering Heights* by Emily Brontë

You are of such value to me that all else has become naught. You are my heart, my life, my one and only thought . . . I cannot live without you, I cannot leave you without a word of love. All is changed to me since I have known you. I am poor and lowly and all unworthy of you; but if great love may weigh down such defects, then mine may do it. Give me but one word of hope to take to the wars with me—but one.

From *The White Company* by Sir Arthur Conan Doyle

MARY AND PERCY SHELLEY

Percy and Mary Shelley, the author of *Frankenstein*, were both renowned writers, even if perhaps not in their own times, who truly put the "hopeless" in "hopeless romantics." They met when Percy began frequently visiting Mary's father, whose political philosophy he admired. The young lovers would secretly meet each other at the grave of Mary's mother, where during one rendezvous they declared their love for each other.

The two eloped and began traveling Europe together. These travels included an extended stay at the Geneva home of the poet Lord Byron. During their stay, Byron proposed that each come up with a ghost story, which ultimately inspired Mary to start writing what would later become *Frankenstein*. Percy greatly encouraged Mary's writing of her great gothic novel, for which he wrote the forward.

Unfortunately, Mary and Percy's time together would come to an end just a few years later when in 1822 Percy died in a boating accident, after which his body was cremated on the very beach it washed up upon. Mary was heartbroken, but continued Percy's legacy for the rest of her life by promoting his writings on philosophy and his poetry until her own death in 1851. One year after Mary's death, her only surviving child, Percy Florence Shelley, discovered that Mary had kept the calcified heart of Percy delicately wrapped in silk and pages of his poetry within her writing desk for all the years they were parted by the grave.

Love gives naught but itself and takes naught but from itself.
Love possesses not nor would it be possessed;
For love is sufficient unto love.
When you love you should not say, "God is in my heart,"
but rather, "I am in the heart of God."
And think not you can direct the course of love, for love,
if it finds you worthy, directs your course.
Love has no other desire but to fulfill itself.

From *The Prophet* by Khalil Gibran

But eager love denies the least delay.
Let softer cares the present hour employ,
And be these moments sacred all to joy.
Never did my soul so strong a passion prove,
Or for an earthly, or a heavenly love;

From *The Iliad* by Homer

The angel and apostle of the coming revelation must be a woman, indeed, but lofty, pure, and beautiful; and wise, moreover, not through dusky grief, but the ethereal medium of joy; and showing how sacred love should make us happy, by the truest test of a life successful to such an end!

From *The Scarlet Letter* by Nathaniel Hawthorne

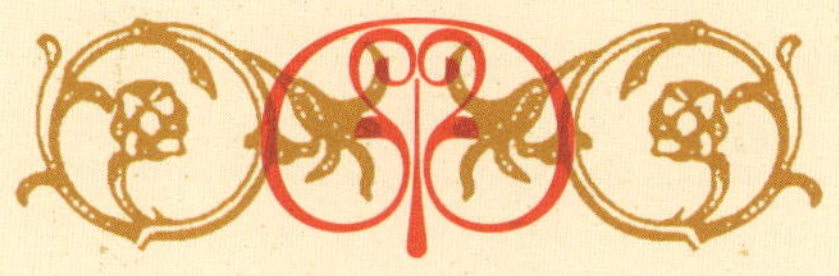

Your fear, your terror, all of that is just love and love of the most exquisite kind, the kind which people do not admit even to themselves, the kind that gives you a thrill, when you think of it . . .

From *The Phantom of the Opera* by Gaston Leroux

I have for the first time found what I can truly love—I have found you. You are my sympathy—my better self—my good angel. I am bound to you with a strong attachment. I think you good, gifted, lovely: a fervent, a solemn passion is conceived in my heart; it leans to you, draws you to my center and spring of life, wraps my existence about you, and, kindling in pure, powerful flame, fuses you and me in one.

From *Jane Eyre* by Charlotte Brontë

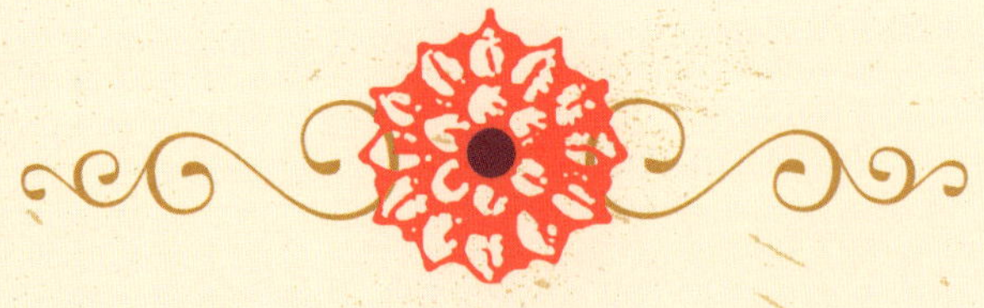

I confess to you, my friend, that I love you and that in my airy dreams of futurity you have been my constant friend and companion. But it is your happiness I desire as well as my own when I declare to you that our marriage would render me eternally miserable unless it were the dictate of your own free choice.

From *Frankenstein* by Mary Shelley

I ought not to doubt the steadiness of your affection, yet such is the inconsistency of real love, that it is always awake to suspicion, however unreasonable; always requiring new assurances from the object of its interest, and thus it is, that I always feel revived, as by a new conviction, when your words tell me I am dear to you; and wanting these, I relapse into doubt, and often into despondency.

From *The Mysteries of Udolpho* by Ann Radcliffe

You will think me cruel, very selfish, but love is always selfish; the more ardent the more selfish. How jealous I am you cannot know. You must come with me, loving me, to death; or else hate me and still come with me, and hating me through death and after. There is no such word as indifference in my apathetic nature.

From *Carmilla* by J. Sheridan Le Fanu

"What are you coming for?" she said, letting fall the hand with which she had grasped the door post. And irrepressible delight and eagerness shone in her face.

"What am I coming for?" he repeated, looking straight into her eyes. "You know that I have come to be where you are, I can't help it."

From *Anna Karenina* by Leo Tolstoy

I loved her simply because I found her irresistible . . . I knew to my sorrow, often and often, if not always, that I loved her against reason, against promise, against peace, against hope, against happiness, against all discouragement that could be . . . I loved her nonetheless because I knew it, and it had no more influence in restraining me than if I had devoutly believed her to be human perfection.

From *Great Expectations* by Charles Dickens

LASZLO CRAVENSWORTH AND NADJA OF ANTIPAXOS

Laszlo and Nadja from the FX television series *What We Do in the Shadows* maintain a marriage that would cause anyone envy, though admittedly they have plenty of practice after centuries at each other's side. Residing in Staten Island, New York, with two other roommates, Nadja and Laszlo spend their nights romping around the island searching for their next victims, wearing matching outfits, and enjoying all the delights of immortal life. Over hundreds of years together, the two have cultivated an intimate understanding of each other, as well as many shared experiences and private jokes, and are still just as infatuated with each other as the night they met.

Protective but not possessive of each other, these two are truly secure in their relationship and they feel free to explore outside their relationship, knowing that their partner will always be there for them. While like any couple they have the occasional spat or quarrel—though perhaps with more hissing than average—they always manage to navigate their conflicts together.

Another testament to their unshakable bond, Laszlo and Nadja have no problem poking fun at each other while remaining supportive of each other's interests, dreams, and ambitions. These two would do just about anything for each other, whether that's finding new ways to spice up their relationship even after centuries together or beheading anyone that makes their beloved cry. While their distinctive fashion tastes and accents may be a bit dated, their love is truly eternal.

Adieu, my love! Write often to your poor girl and write long letters; for I not only like them for being longer, but because more heart steals into them; and I am happy to catch your heart whenever I can.

From Letter XV from Mary Wollstonecraft to Gilbert Imlay

They gave a love that grew with their growth, and bound them tenderly together by the sweetest tie which blesses life and outlives death.

From *Little Women* by Louisa May Alcott

I have no notion of loving people by halves; it is not my nature.

From *Northanger Abbey* by Jane Austen

I did not know how the love of a woman will tinge a man's whole life and every action with unselfishness. I did not know how easy it is to be noble when someone else takes it for granted that one will be so; or how wide and interesting life becomes when viewed by four eyes instead of two. I had much to learn, you see; but I think I have learned it.

From *The Stark Munro Letters* by Sir Arthur Conan Doyle

His hand took hold of hers, and as she said something low in his ear he turned toward her with a rush of emotion. I think that voice held him most, with its fluctuating, feverish warmth, because it couldn't be over-dreamed—that voice was a deathless song.

From *The Great Gatsby* by F. Scott Fitzgerald

Though I had now given up all hope of seeing you, I could not resolve to tear myself from a place so near to you . . . O how heavily the moments have passed, yet with what various emotion have they been marked, as I sometimes thought I heard footsteps, and fancied you were approaching, and then again—perceived only a dead and dreary silence! But, when you opened the door of the pavilion, and the darkness prevented my distinguishing with certainty, whether it was my love—my heart beat so strongly with hopes and fears, that I could not speak.

From *The Mysteries of Udolpho* by Ann Radcliffe

LET US LIVE
THE MOST
DELICIOUS LIFE
AND DEVOUR IT
TOGETHER
Unknown Author

SOUL

MATES

Bound by fate, pulled together by something more than just physical attraction, a clever tongue, and proximity, soulmates share an intense bond that amplifies their love. Often one cannot live without the other.

Nelly, I am Heathcliff! He's always, always in my mind: not as a pleasure, any more than I am always a pleasure to myself, but as my own being. So don't talk of our separation again: it is impracticable.

From *Wuthering Heights* by Emily Brontë

But it was as if I had been looking at him for years and had known him always . . .

From *The Turn of the Screw* by Henry James

We have now little time to waste in exclamation, or assertion, if you are yet to learn how dear you are, and ever must be, to my heart, no assurances of mine can give you conviction.

From *The Mysteries of Udolpho* by Ann Radcliffe

No sign of love does it require to seek for, there; For love is love's own sign, given from the highest sphere.

From *The Mesnevi* by Rumi

There is no happiness like that of being loved by your fellow creatures, and feeling that your presence is an addition to their comfort.

From *Jane Eyre* by Charlotte Brontë

No man is offended by another man's admiration of the woman he loves; it is the woman only who can make it a torment.

From *Northanger Abbey* by Jane Austen

Ever since I first looked upon your wonderful and incomparable beauty, I have dared to love you wildly, passionately, devotedly, hopelessly.

From *The Importance of Being Earnest* by Oscar Wilde

I must have you for my own—entirely my own. Will you be mine? Say yes, quickly.

From *Jane Eyre* by Charlotte Brontë

And you, their best beloved one, are now to me, flesh of my flesh; blood of my blood; kin of my kin; my bountiful wine-press for a while; and shall be later on my companion and my helper.

From *Dracula* by Bram Stoker

I have been in love with no one, and never shall . . . unless it should be with you.

From *Carmilla* by J. Sheridan Le Fanu

When I was very young, I set before myself the ideal of the woman I loved and should be happy to call my wife. I have lived through a long life, and now for the first time I have met what I sought—in you. I love you, and offer you my hand.

From *Anna Karenina* by Leo Tolstoy

ALL OF THE WORST PARTS OF ME LOVE THE WORST PARTS OF YOU

Unknown Author

I cannot express it; but surely you and everybody have a notion that there is or should be an existence of yours beyond you.

From *Wuthering Heights* by Emily Brontë

He was in love and his love was returned. Turning on all the lights, he looked at himself in the mirror, trying to find in his own face the qualities that made him see clearer than the great crowd of people, that made him decide firmly, and able to influence and follow his own will.

From *This Side of Paradise* by F. Scott Fitzgerald

"How inflexible you are! You would draw love down to the level of physics."
"Or draw physics up to the level of love."

From "A Physiologist's Wife" by Sir Arthur Conan Doyle

GOMEZ AND MORTICIA ADDAMS

Gomez and Morticia are far from the conventional couple, but their spooky souls are most definitely meant for each other. These two love bats, and the rest of their brood (who they love just as much), spend their days tangoing and scheming around their gothic mansion atop a gloomy hill. Perhaps even more intimidating and dramatic than their home are the Addamses themselves. Gomez is stocky and brimming with passion, not to mention always immaculately dressed and groomed in dark suits with particular attention paid to his mustache. The ethereal, statuesque Morticia, clad in her slinky, jet-black dresses, always manages to catch the light *just right* and possesses an otherworldly calmness reserved for those that don't fear the grave.

While their neighbors might call them freaks—which the Addamses would only take as a compliment, thank you very much—Gomez and Morticia enjoy a truly blissful relationship. They are utterly dedicated to each other; Gomez would challenge the sun itself to a swordfight to win his beloved a few more minutes of beauty sleep (not that she needs it of course) and Morticia can read her husband's moods like the lines in her own palms. Even after years of marriage and multiple children, they still manage to keep the spark—or more accurately the bonfire—between them alive. Gomez and Morticia are nothing less than completely their creepy and kooky selves, and don't shy away from treasuring even the darkest and most depraved parts of their partner.

O Loveliness, return,
Make once again my soul to sing in joy,
Feed once again this heart with fires that burn, Gods!

From *Sappho: A New Rendering* translated by H. de Vere Stacpool

My only love sprung from my only hate!
Too early seen unknown, and known too late!
Prodigious birth of love it is to me,
That I must love a loathed enemy.

From *Romeo and Juliet* by William Shakespeare

Give your hearts, but not into each other's keeping.
For only the hand of Life can contain your hearts.
And stand together yet not too near together.

From *The Prophet* by Khalil Gibran

This love which I had thought was a joke and a plaything—it is only now that I understand that it is the molder of one's life, the most solemn and sacred of all things.

From *The Adventures of Gerard* by Sir Arthur Conan Doyle

I have touched you, heard you, felt the comfort of your presence—the sweetness of your consolation: I cannot give up these joys. I have little left in myself—I must have you. The world may laugh—may call me absurd, selfish—but it does not signify. My very soul demands you: it will be satisfied, or it will take deadly vengeance on its frame.

From *Jane Eyre* by Charlotte Brontë

I pray every night that I may live after him; because I would rather be miserable than that he should be: that proves I love him better than myself.

From *Wuthering Heights* by Emily Brontë

He did not care if she was heartless, vicious and vulgar, stupid and grasping, he loved her. He would rather have misery with the one than happiness with the other.

From *Of Human Bondage* by W. Somerset Maugham

Alas! . . . It was love; love, the comfort of the human species, the preserver of the universe, the soul of all sensible beings, love, tender love.

From *Candide* by Voltaire

But if you wish me to love you, could you but see how much I do love you, you would be proud and content. All my heart is yours, sir: it belongs to you; and with you it would remain, were fate to exile the rest of me from your presence forever.

From *Jane Eyre* by Charlotte Brontë

The souls love-moved are circling on,
Like streams to their great Ocean King.
Thou art the Sun of all men's thoughts;
Thy kisses are the flowers of spring.
The dawn is pale from yearning Love;
The moon in tears is sorrowing.
Thou art the Rose, and deep for Thee,
In sighs, the nightingales still sing.

From "The Souls Love-Moved" by Rumi

Since with its beam
The grace, whence true love lighteth first his flame,
That after doth increase by loving, shines.

From *The Divine Comedy* by Dante Alighieri

There was something between them.
There was everything.

From *The Turn of the Screw* by Henry James

Perhaps, after all, romance did not come into one's life with pomp and blare, like a gay knight riding down; perhaps it crept to one's side like an old friend through quiet ways; perhaps it revealed itself in seeming prose, until some sudden shaft of illumination flung athwart its pages betrayed the rhythm and the music, perhaps . . . perhaps . . . love unfolded naturally out of a beautiful friendship, as a golden-hearted rose slipping from its green sheath.

From *Anne of Avonlea* by L. M. Montgomery

Love can be monstrous under terrible circumstances, but we are at the whims of our spirit. Ethereal and demonic creatures show a love that outpaces the mundane, and the romantic allure of the supernatural is undeniable.

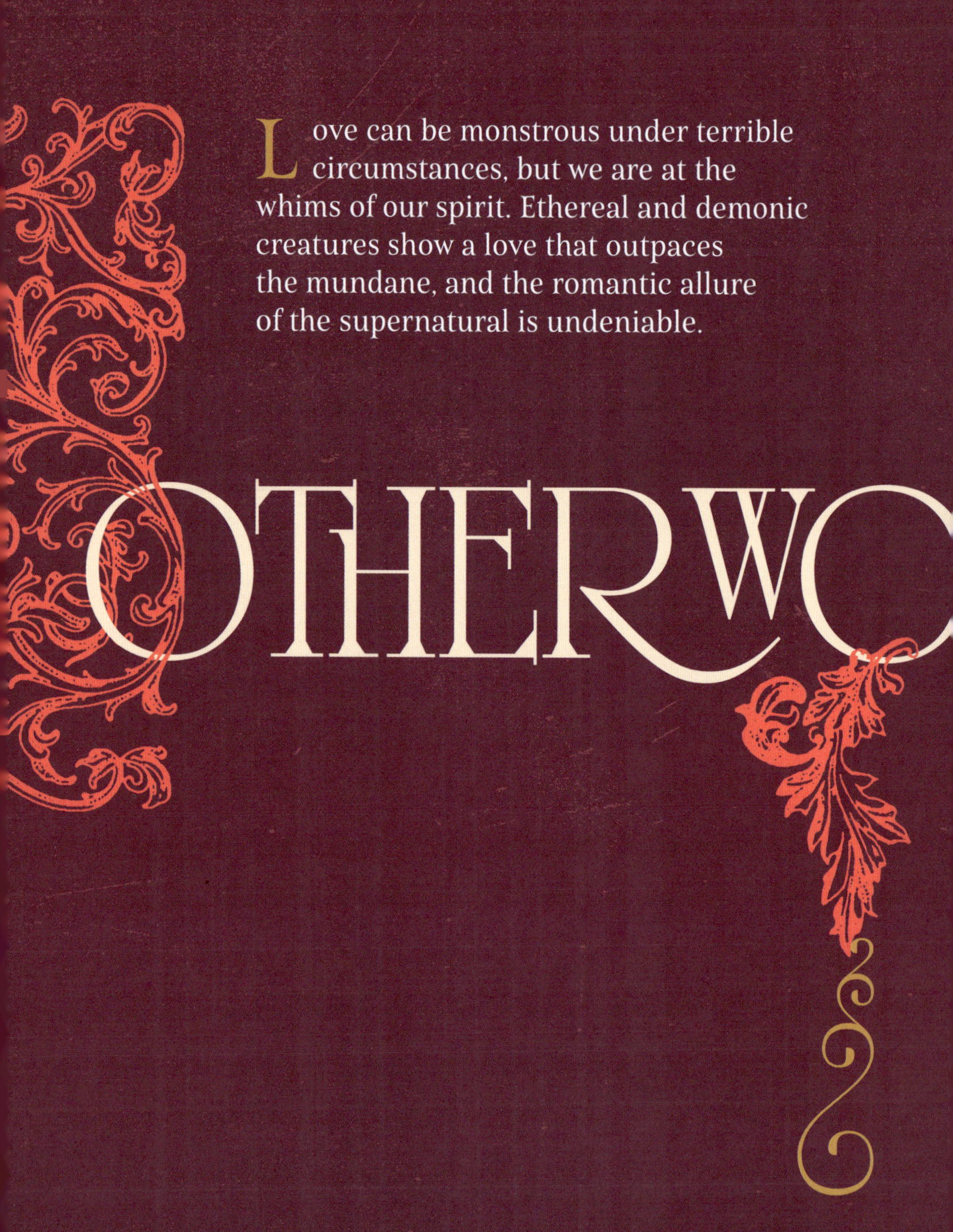

RLDLINESS

It is true, we shall be monsters, cut off from all the world; but on that account we shall be more attached to one another.

From *Frankenstein* by Mary Shelley

Every heart has its own skeletons.

From *Anna Karenina* by Leo Tolstoy

You are nearest and dearest and all the world to me; our souls are knit into one, for all life and all time.

From *Dracula* by Bram Stoker

There is real love just as there are real ghosts; every person speaks of it, few persons have seen it.

From *Reflections; or Sentences and Moral Maxims*
by Francois de La Rouchefoucauld

You—you strange, you almost unearthly thing!—I love as my own flesh.

From *Jane Eyre* by Charlotte Brontë

The heavens torn asunder and an angel's voice heard upon earth for the delight of mankind and the utter capture of his heart.

From *The Phantom of the Opera* by Gaston Leroux

Love has been taken away from the poets, and has been brought within the domain of true science. It may prove to be one of the great cosmic elementary forces. When the atom of hydrogen draws the atom of chlorine towards it to form the perfected molecule of hydrochloric acid, the force which it exerts may be intrinsically similar to that which draws me to you. Attraction and repulsion appear to be the primary forces.
This is attraction.

From "A Physiologist's Wife" by Sir Arthur Conan Doyle

How eloquent are eyes!
Not the rapt poet's frenzied lay
When the soul's wildest feelings stray
Can speak so well as they.
How eloquent are eyes!
Not music's most impassioned note
On which Love's warmest fervors float
Like them bids rapture rise.

Love, look thus again, –
That your look may light a waste of years,
Darting the beam that conquers cares
Through the cold shower of tears.
Love, look thus again!

"Eyes: A Fragment" by Percy Bysshe Shelley

Nay, without thought or conscious desire, might not things external to ourselves vibrate in unison with our moods and passions, atom calling to atom in secret love or strange affinity?

From *The Picture of Dorian Gray* by Oscar Wilde

My heart, which was before sorrowful, now swelled with something like joy; I exclaimed, "Wandering spirits, if indeed ye wander, and do not rest in your narrow beds, allow me this faint happiness, or take me, as your companion, away from the joys of life."

From *Frankenstein* by Mary Shelley

Haunt me, then! The murdered do haunt their murderers, I believe. I know that ghosts have wandered on earth. Be with me always—take any form—drive me mad! Only do not leave me in this abyss, where I cannot find you! Oh, God! it is unutterable! I cannot live without my life! I cannot live without my soul!

From *Wuthering Heights* by Emily Brontë

That I did always love,
I bring thee proof:
That till I loved
I did not love enough.

That I shall love always,
I offer thee
That love is life,
And life hath immortality.

This, dost thou doubt, sweet?
Then have I
Nothing to show
But Calvary.

"Proof" by Emily Dickinson

Love will have its sacrifices. No sacrifice without blood.

From *Carmilla* by J. Sheridan Le Fanu

No amount of fire or freshness can challenge what a man can store up in his ghostly heart.

From *The Great Gatsby* by F. Scott Fitzgerald

I have something in my brain and heart, in my blood and nerves, that assimilates me mentally to him.

From *Jane Eyre* by Charlotte Brontë

Of all ghosts the ghosts of our old lovers are the worst.

From *The Memoirs of Sherlock Holmes*
by Sir Arthur Conan Doyle

The forms of the beloved dead flit before me, and I hasten to their arms.

From *Frankenstein* by Mary Shelley

I love you with all my heart, but my soul is still full of fright at that which I have seen and experienced.

From *Candide* by Voltaire

This little star is furnish'd with good spirits,
Whose mortal lives were busied to that end,
That honor and renown might wait on them:
And, when desires thus err in their intention,
True love must needs ascend with slacker beam.

From *The Divine Comedy* by Dante Alighieri

Love is the astrolabe of God's mysteries.
A lover may hanker after this love or that love,
But at the last he is drawn to the KING of Love.
However much we describe and explain Love,
When we fall in love we are ashamed of our words.
Explanation by the tongue makes most things clear,
But Love unexplained is better.

From "Description of Love" by Rumi

Thrill my heart that throbs with unwonted fervor,
Chasten mouth and throat with immortal kisses,
Till I yield on maddening heights the very
Breath of my body.

From "The Muses" by Sappho

The sacred name of his love had sprung from his heart and his lips. He could not keep it back . . . He would have given anything to withdraw it, for that name, proclaimed in the stillness of the night, had acted as though it were the preconcerted signal for a furious rush . . .

From *The Phantom of the Opera* by Gaston Leroux

I could feel the soft, shivering touch of the lips on the super-sensitive skin of my throat, and the hard dents of two sharp teeth, just touching and pausing there. I closed my eyes in a languorous ecstasy and waited—waited with beating heart.

From *Dracula* by Bram Stoker

LISA SWALLOWS AND THE CREATURE

What could an angsty teenager mourning the death of her mother and the corpse of a young Victorian man killed by a lightning strike possibly have in common? Apparently quite a bit, if Lisa Swallows and The Creature from 2024's *Lisa Frankenstein* are any evidence. Lisa is a high schooler who, traumatized by her mother's murder, suffers from partial mutism and withdraws from those around her. Instead, she finds comfort in visiting and tending the grave of a Victorian man in an abandoned and overgrown cemetery in the forest.

After some miscommunications, the two form a very close bond as Lisa finds herself able to talk to The Creature. The Creature in turn becomes quite protective of Lisa, which escalates in him killing Lisa's cruel stepmother. However, there's nothing like revenge (and a little electrocution from a malfunctioning tanning bed) to ignite the spark of young love, as Lisa and The Creature discover they can attach body parts from the recently living to restore some of The Creature's humanity. Naturally, they go on a murder spree to collect parts for The Creature and get revenge on those who hurt Lisa, all while falling in love. But all good things must come to an end, and Lisa instructs The Creature to burn her alive in the tanning bed after one last kiss. Thankfully, lightning does in fact strike twice, and their reanimated corpses get to enjoy a lovely gothic existence for the rest of eternity, together.

DEVO

UNTO

TION

True romance is unwavering loyalty bestowed even in the face of mortality. A heart that beats for their one and only until it beats no more. You can love someone to death and beyond, if your love is eternal and pure.

DEATH

Take this kiss upon the brow!
And, in parting from you now,
Thus much let me avow:
You are not wrong, who deem
That my days have been a dream;
Yet if hope has flown away
In a night, or in a day,
In a vision, or in none,
Is it therefore the less gone?
All that we see or seem
Is but a dream within a dream.

From "A Dream Within a Dream" by Edgar Allan Poe

"Does he love you so much?"
"He would commit murder for me."

From *The Phantom of the Opera* by Gaston Leroux

You know nothing about me, and nothing about the sort of love of which I am capable. Every atom of your flesh is as dear to me as my own: in pain and sickness it would still be dear. Your mind is my treasure, and if it were broken, it would be my treasure still.

From *Jane Eyre* by Charlotte Brontë

Death that hath suck'd the honey of thy breath,
Hath had no power yet upon thy beauty.
Thou art not conquer'd. Beauty's ensign yet
Is crimson in thy lips and in thy cheeks,
And death's pale flag is not advanced there.

From *Romeo and Juliet* by William Shakespeare

Love is anterior to life,
Posterior to death,
Initial of creation, and
The exponent of breath.

"Love" by Emily Dickinson

F
FROM
FIRST KISS
TO
LAST BREATH
Unknown Author

I love you very tenderly. Remember me with affection, should you never hear from me again.

From *Frankenstein* by Mary Shelley

But to die as lovers may—to die together, so that they may live together.

From *Carmilla* by J. Sheridan Le Fanu

I love the fair Lady Maude, and would give the last drop of my heart's blood to serve her.

From *The White Company* by Sir Arthur Conan Doyle

The curtains were half drawn, the floor was swept
And strewn with rushes, rosemary and may
Lay thick upon the bed on which I lay,
Where through the lattice ivy-shadows crept.
He leaned above me, thinking that I slept
And could not hear him; but I heard him say,
'Poor child, poor child': and as he turned away
Came a deep silence, and I knew he wept.
He did not touch the shroud, or raise the fold
That hid my face, or take my hand in his,
Or ruffle the smooth pillows for my head:
He did not love me living; but once dead
He pitied me; and very sweet it is
To know he still is warm though I am cold.

"After Death" by Christina Rossetti

CATHERINE EARNSHAW AND HEATHCLIFF

Despite the 1847 publication of Emily Brontë's classic novel *Wuthering Heights*, there have been very few couples, either real or fictional, that can match the intensity of the passion shared between Heathcliff and Catherine Earnshaw. Heathcliff and Catherine first meet when Catherine's father adopts Heathcliff and brings him home to be Catherine and her brother Hindley's adoptive sibling. Catherine and Heathcliff soon develop a deep and intense relationship, with the two spending much of their time together wandering the expansive moors of the Wuthering Heights estate. However, their carefree days of infatuation come to an end when Mr. Earnshaw dies and Hindley inherits Wuthering Heights, demoting Heathcliff to little more than a servant and eventually forbidding him to see Catherine.

Their love, despite its intensity, is purely emotional, to the point that it borders on the spiritual. Catherine and Heathcliff understand each other better than anyone else in existence, and at times better than they seem to understand themselves. However, despite their love for each other, Catherine accepts the marriage proposal of a wealthy neighbor, believing Heathcliff's low social class would drag them both down in life. Heathcliff learns of Catherine's engagement and becomes distraught, fleeing from Wuthering Heights without a word. He returns many years later to seek revenge on those who prevented him and Catherine from being together, and he and Catherine continue to experience a longing for each other that nears on desperation, and when ultimately denied drives both Heathcliff and Catherine down dark and destructive paths.

Hear then; and as in fate and love we join,
Ah, suffer that my bones may rest with thine!
Together have we lived, together bred,
One house received us, and one table fed:
That golden urn, thy goddess-mother gave,
May mix our ashes in one common grave.

From *The Iliad* by Homer

Two words would comprehend my future—death and hell: existence, after losing her, would be hell.

From *Wuthering Heights* by Emily Brontë

Once, someone who had terribly loved him had written to him a mad letter, ending with these idolatrous words: "The world is changed because you are made of ivory and gold. The curves of your lips rewrite history."

From *The Picture of Dorian Gray* by Oscar Wilde

Love her, love her, love her! If she favors you, love her. If she wounds you, love her. If she tears your heart to pieces—and as it gets older and stronger it will tear deeper—love her, love her, love her!

From *Great Expectations* by Charles Dickens

Love, that in gentle heart is quickly learnt,
Entangled him by that fair form, from me
Ta'en in such cruel sort, as grieves me still:
Love, that denial takes from none belov'd,
Caught me with pleasing him so passing well,
That, as thou see'st, he yet deserts me not.

Love brought us to one death: Caina waits
The soul, who spilt our life.

From *The Divine Comedy* by Dante Alighieri

Now Love has bound me, trembling, hands and feet,
O Love so fatal, Love so bitter-sweet.

"The Captive" by Sappho

In spite of death, he felt the need of life and love. He felt that love saved him from despair, and that this love, under the menace of despair, had become still stronger and purer. The one mystery of death, still unsolved, had scarcely passed before his eyes, when another mystery had arisen, as insoluble, urging him to love and to life.

From *Anna Karenina* by Leo Tolstoy

VICTOR VAN DORT, VICTORIA EVERGLOT, AND EMILY

Victoria, Victor, and Emily from the 2005 animated film *Tim Burton's Corpse Bride* take "until death do us part" to the extreme. Victor, a drearily dressed, timid, and good-natured young man is betrothed to the equally pallid and darkly clothed Victoria. While initially hesitant about their impending marriage, they quickly bond over their shared love of melancholic piano music and fall in love. However, the clumsy Victor ruins their vow rehearsal, after which he goes to sulk in the graveyard and practice his vows and accidently proposes to a "corpse bride" named Emily. Overjoyed, Emily, who was murdered on her wedding night, drags Victor to the surprisingly lively land of the dead.

While Emily immediately falls for Victor, Victor still longs for his original betrothed. Victoria's hold on Victor's heart is only shaken when Victor hears of her marriage to another man, which in his dejection causes him to promise to marry Emily. However, once Victor learns the truth—that Victoria was wed against her will to Emily's murderer—he defends Victoria valiantly in a duel, and with help from Emily, triumphs and frees Victoria. While happy to be reunited with Victoria, Victor attempts to honor his promise to marry Emily, but she lets Victor go to be with the one he truly loves. These three teach us that love is more than just devotion. It is sacrifice.

Know that I am built up of death from head to foot and that it is a corpse that loves you and adores you and will never, never leave you!

From *The Phantom of the Opera* by Gaston Leroux

If she be all tenderness, she will die. If she survive, the tenderness will either be crushed out of her, or—and the outward semblance is the same—crushed so deeply into her heart that it can never show itself more. The latter is perhaps the truest theory.

From *The Scarlet Letter* by Nathaniel Hawthorne

Come gentle night, come loving black-brow'd night,
Give me my Romeo, and when he shall die,
Take him and cut him out in little stars,
And he will make the face of heaven so fine
That all the world will be in love with night,
And pay no worship to the garish sun.
O, I have bought the mansion of a love,
But not possess'd it; and though I am sold,
Not yet enjoy'd.

From *Romeo and Juliet* by William Shakespeare

Look on me, for thou art my companion in the grave
On the night when thou shalt pass from shop and dwelling.
Thou shalt hear my hail in the hollow of the tomb:
it shall become known to thee
That thou wasn't never concealed from mine eye.
I am as reason and intellect within thy bosom
At the time of joy and gladness, at the time
of sorrow and distress.

From "Divine Friend" by Rumi

Could there be anything more dreadful in life than to have those whom you love looking to you for help and to be unable to give it?

From *The Stark Munro Letters* by Sir Arthur Conan Doyle

If all else perished, and he remained, I should still continue to be; and if all else remained, and he were annihilated, the universe would turn to a mighty stranger: I should not seem a part of it.

From *Wuthering Heights* by Emily Brontë

T
TOGETHER
FOREVER,
UNTIL
WE'RE NAMES
ON A TOMBSTONE
Unknown Author

. . . For when I say that I am of his kind, I do not mean that I have his force to influence, and his spell to attract; I mean only that I have certain tastes and feelings in common with him. I must, then, repeat continually that we are forever sundered:—and yet, while I breathe and think, I must love him.

From *Jane Eyre* by Charlotte Brontë

A gentle story of two lovers young,
Who met in innocence and died in sorrow,
And of one selfish heart, whose rancor clung
Like curses on them; are ye slow to borrow
The lore of truth from such a tale?
Or in this world's deserted vale,
Do ye not see a star of gladness
Pierce the shadows of its sadness, —
When ye are cold, that love is a light sent
From Heaven, which none shall quench, to cheer the innocent?

"The Fragment: A Gentle Story of Two Lovers Young"
by Percy Bysshe Shelley

NATUR
AS A M
OF

E

The moon may love the sun and bask in her warmth while never knowing the tenderness of her touch. Likewise, the storm may love the sky only to ruin him with the power of her affection. Both beauty and devastation exist in love as they do, at times with great intensity, in the natural world.

IRROR

LOVE

My bounty is as boundless as the sea,
My love as deep; the more I give to thee,
The more I have, for both are infinite.

From *Romeo and Juliet* by William Shakespeare

Romance, who loves to nod and sing,
With drowsy head and folded wing,
Among the green leaves as they shake
Far down within some shadowy lake,
To me a painted paroquet
Hath been—a most familiar bird—
Taught me my alphabet to say—
To lisp my very earliest word
While in the wild wood I did lie,
A child—with a most knowing eye.

From "Romance" by Edgar Allan Poe

He loved the soothing hour, when the last tints of light die away; when the stars, one by one, tremble through ether, and are reflected on the dark mirror of the waters; that hour, which, of all others, inspires the mind with pensive tenderness, and often elevates it to sublime contemplation.

From *The Mysteries of Udolpho* by Ann Radcliffe

He walked down, for a long while avoiding looking at her as at the sun, but seeing her, as one does the sun, without looking.

From *Anna Karenina* by Leo Tolstoy

*"Are you very much in love with him?"
he asked.*

She did not answer for some time, but stood gazing at the landscape. "I wish I knew," she said at last.

He shook his head. "Knowledge would be fatal. It is the uncertainty that charms one. A mist makes things wonderful."

From *The Picture of Dorian Gray* by Oscar Wilde

Oh, you are indeed there, my skylark! Come to me. You are not gone: not vanished? I heard one of your kind an hour ago, singing high over the wood: but its song had no music for me, any more than the rising sun had rays. All the melody on earth is concentrated in my Jane's tongue to my ear (I am glad it is not naturally a silent one): all the sunshine I can feel is in her presence.

From *Jane Eyre* by Charlotte Brontë

The green woods and pastures; the flowery turf; the blue concave of the heavens; the balmy air; the murmur of the limpid stream; and even the hum of every little insect of the shade, seem to revivify the soul, and make mere existence bliss.

From *The Mysteries of Udolpho* by Ann Radcliffe

Unknown Author

He knew she was there by the rapture and the terror that seized on his heart. She was standing talking to a lady at the opposite end of the ground. There was apparently nothing striking either in her dress or her attitude. But for Levin she was as easy to find in that crowd as a rose among nettles. Everything was made bright by her.

From *Anna Karenina* by Leo Tolstoy

Let us look again for a moment; it is the last time, perhaps, I shall see the moonlight with you.

From *Carmilla* by J. Sheridan Le Fanu

I am longing to be with you, and by the sea, where we can talk together freely and build our castles in the air.

From *Dracula* by Bram Stoker

But his heart was in a constant, turbulent riot. The most grotesque and fantastic conceits haunted him in his bed at night. A universe of ineffable gaudiness spun itself out in his brain while the clock ticked on the washstand and the moon soaked with wet light his tangled clothes upon the floor.

From *The Great Gatsby* by F. Scott Fitzgerald

When you are inquisitive, Jane, you always make me smile. You open your eyes like an eager bird, and make every now and then a restless movement, as if answers in speech did not flow fast enough for you, and you wanted to read the tablet of one's heart. But before I go on, tell me what you mean by your 'Well, sir?' It is a small phrase very frequent with you; and which many a time has drawn me on and on through interminable talk: I don't very well know why.

From *Jane Eyre* by Charlotte Brontë

EDWARD SCISSORHANDS AND KIM

Edward and Kim from the 1990 film *Edward Scissorhands* capture the innocence and troubles of young love and the bond that is formed when someone sees you for who you truly are, regardless of your flaws and sharp edges. Edward, the scissor-handed creation of an inventor, cuts an intimidating figure with spiky black hair, pale face, a leather-clad body, and his namesake blades. But despite his appearance, Edward is sweet, timid, and gentle, even with his particular set of appendages. The less radically-adorned Kim is a fairly average teenage girl: She goes camping, participates in cheerleading, and is frightened to find Edward sleeping in her bed after her mother "rescues" him from his gothic mansion. Edward falls in love with Kim on first seeing her picture and is utterly devoted to her from the start.

Edward expresses his affection, both for Kim and the greater community, utilizing his abundant creativity and his hands to reflect the natural beauty of the world. While his talents make him popular around suburbia, Kim appreciates Edward as a full-fledged person instead of as a novelty, or as a danger when the neighborhood later turns on him. Kim falls for Edward after realizing his true devotion to her, and she helps him escape back to his inventor's mansion. After one tragic kiss she leaves him there forever, convincing the neighborhood that he died in order to keep him safe. But Edward most certainly remembers her, carving his cherished memories out of ice and blanketing the neighborhood in the snow that Kim loves.

. . . the longer the days are, the more distant is the sun, and nevertheless the hotter; so is it with our love, for by absence we are kept a distance from one another, and yet it retains its fervour, at least on my side.

From Henry VIII's fourth love letter to Anne Boleyn

Love, whether newly born, or aroused from a death-like slumber, must always create a sunshine, filling the heart so full of radiance, that it overflows upon the outward world.

From *The Scarlet Letter* by Nathaniel Hawthorne

When he stepped out onto the grass, he drew a deep breath. The fresh morning air seemed to drive away all his somber passions. He thought only of Sibyl. A faint echo of his love came back to him. He repeated her name over and over again. The birds that were singing in the dew-drenched garden seemed to be telling the flowers about her.

From *The Picture of Dorian Gray* by Oscar Wilde

When the moon shed her soft rays among the foliage, he still lingered, and his pastoral supper of cream and fruits was often spread beneath it. Then, on the stillness of night, came the song of the nightingale, breathing sweetness, and awakening melancholy.

From *The Mysteries of Udolpho* by Ann Radcliffe

Thou art of all Man's Joys the Spring;
Life's honey'd Sweetness thou dost bring.
My gather'd Pearls, from Bosom full,
Before thy Feet my glad Hands fling.
The Souls love-moved, are circling on,
Like Streams to their great Ocean King.
Thou art the Sun of all Men's Thoughts;
Thy Kisses are the Flowers of Spring.
The Dawn is pale from yearning Love;
The Moon in Tears is sorrowing.
Thou art the Rose; and deep for thee,
In Sighs, the Nightingales still sing.
O can my Love me so despise,
That he my Heart with Pain can wring?
O Wine of Life, all fragrant, pour,
And soothe the Pain of Death's last Sting!

"The First and Last" by Rumi

It was not the thorn bending to the honeysuckles, but the honeysuckles embracing the thorn. There were no mutual concessions: one stood erect, and the others yielded: and who can be ill-natured and bad-tempered when they encounter neither opposition nor indifference?

From *Wuthering Heights* by Emily Brontë

No man knows till he has suffered from the night how sweet and how dear to his heart and eye the morning can be.

From *Dracula* by Bram Stoker

He looked at her as a man looks at a faded flower he has gathered, with difficulty recognizing in it the beauty for which he picked and ruined it. And in spite of this he felt that then, when his love was stronger, he could, if he had greatly wished it, have torn that love out of his heart; but now, when as at that moment it seemed to him he felt no love for her, he knew that what bound him to her could not be broken.

From *Anna Karenina* by Leo Tolstoy

Love shook my soul as winds on forests blow;
This lawless heart that dared exhaust delight,
Unsated strove and maddened through the night.

From "Ode to Atthis" by Sappho

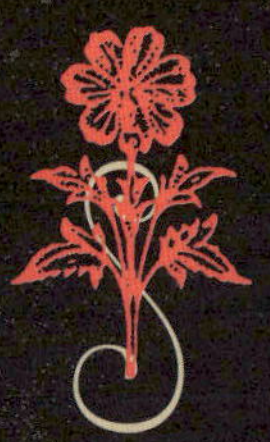

How do I love thee? Let me count the ways.
I love thee to the depth and breadth and height
My soul can reach, when feeling out of sight
For the ends of being and ideal grace.
I love thee to the level of every day's
Most quiet need, by sun and candle-light.
I love thee freely, as men strive for right.
I love thee purely, as they turn from praise.
I love thee with the passion put to use
In my old griefs, and with my childhood's faith.
I love thee with a love I seemed to lose
With my lost saints. I love thee with the breath,
Smiles, tears, of all my life; and, if God choose,
I shall but love thee better after death.

"How Do I Love Thee (Sonnet 43)"
by Elizabeth Barrett Browning

He remembered the autumn that he had passed there, and a wonderful love that had stirred him to mad delightful follies. There was romance in every place.

From *The Picture of Dorian Gray* by Oscar Wilde

Such was the sympathy of Nature—that wild, heathen Nature of the forest, never subjugated by human law, nor illumined by higher truth—with the bliss of these two spirits! Love, whether newly born, or aroused from a death-like slumber, must always create a sunshine, filling the heart so full of radiance, that it overflows upon the outward world.

From *The Scarlet Letter* by Nathaniel Hawthorne

It is to the credit of human nature, that, except where its selfishness is brought into play, it loves more readily than it hates. Hatred, by a gradual and quiet process, will even be transformed to love, unless the change be impeded by a continually new irritation of the original feeling of hostility.

From *The Scarlet Letter* by Nathaniel Hawthorne

There is always some madness in love. But there is always, also, some method in madness.

From *Thus Spake Zarathustra* by Friedrich Nietzsche

I'm not sentimental—I'm as romantic as you are. The idea, you know, is that the sentimental person thinks things will last—the romantic person has a desperate confidence that they won't.

From *This Side of Paradise* by F. Scott Fitzgerald

Love sought is good, but given unsought is better.

From *Twelfth Night* by William Shakespeare

He shall never know how I love him: and that, not because he's handsome, Nelly, but because he's more myself than I am. Whatever our souls are made of, his and mine are the same.

From *Wuthering Heights* by Emily Brontë

Your hearts know in silence the secrets
of the days and the nights.

From *The Prophet* by Khalil Gibran

Her love was trembling in laughter on her lips.

From *The Picture of Dorian Gray* by Oscar Wilde

They put their finger on their lip,
The Powers above:
The seas their islands clip,
The moons in ocean dip,
They love, but name not love.

"Silence" by Ralph Waldo Emerson

Virtue and taste are nearly the same, for virtue is little more than active taste, and the most delicate affections of each combine in real love. How then are we to look for love in great cities, where selfishness, dissipation, and insincerity supply the place of tenderness, simplicity and truth?

From *The Mysteries of Udolpho* by Ann Radcliffe

He had a heart that could have held the entire empire of the world; and, in the end, he had to content himself with a cellar. Ah, yes, we must needs pity the Opera ghost.

From *The Phantom of the Opera* by Gaston Leroux

It requires uncommon steadiness of reason to resist the attraction of being called the most charming girl in the world.

From *Northanger Abbey* by Jane Austen

I turned my lips to the hand that lay on my shoulder. I loved him very much—more than I could trust myself to say—more than words had power to express.

From *Jane Eyre* by Charlotte Brontë

I loved him with a mixture of affection and reverence that knew no bounds, yet I could never persuade myself to confide in him that event which was so often present to my recollection . . .

From *Frankenstein* by Mary Shelley

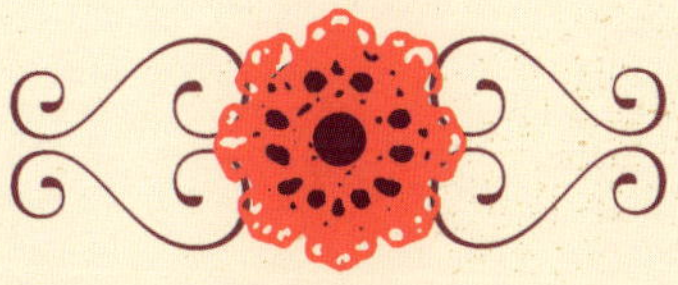

She was so fair to look on, so radiantly beautiful, so exquisitely voluptuous, that the very instinct of man in me, which calls some of my sex to love and to protect one of hers, made my head whirl with new emotion.

From *Dracula* by Bram Stoker

I loved him as one loves for the first time—with idolatry, with transport.

From *Candide* by Voltaire

. . . the element of the unnamed and untouched became, between us, greater than any other . . .

From *The Turn of the Screw* by Henry James

Her murmured words sounded like a lullaby in my ear, and soothed my resistance into a trance, from which I only seemed to recover myself when she withdrew her arms.

From *Carmilla* by J. Sheridan Le Fanu

In dreams our limbs are joined, as flame with flame,
In dreams again your arms are girdling me,
I taste your soul in joys I blush to name.

From *Sappho: A New Rendering*
translated by H. de Vere Stacpool

JACK AND SALLY

Jack and Sally from *Tim Burton's The Nightmare Before Christmas* are one of the most iconic goth couples of all time. Jack, the spidery, black-and-white pinstripe-clad skeleton and Pumpkin King can strike fear into even the bravest of souls. Despite his intimidating persona, Jack has a flair for the dramatic and a tendency to get caught up in his own grand schemes. Sally the rag doll, Jack's stitched-together sweetheart, is a little more down to earth—maybe because her body is stuffed with autumn leaves. Sally, in contrast with Jack's ghoulish charisma, is sweet and a bit shy, but her cleverness, propensity for alchemy, and scary-accurate intuition make her a force to be reckoned with.

Despite Jack's drama, his and Sally's love story is comprised of many small, often unspoken gestures. Whether its Sally's gift of alchemical butterflies or Jack's insistence that Sally is the only one clever enough to design his "Sandy Claws" suit, this paranormal pair share a number of subtle moments that demonstrate their mutual respect and admiration for each other. However, in true goth fashion, this subtlety leaves plenty of room for angst. Sally is prone to longing, voicing her woes to the gloomy fog of the night. But thankfully, Jack puts her doubts to rest atop a snowy hill in a moonlit graveyard, reaffirming that the two of them are simply meant to be. Jack and Sally show us that simple, honest gestures of love and affection can build a foundation that can last an eternity.

Because I sometimes have a queer feeling with regard to you—especially when you are near me, as now: it is as if I had a string somewhere under my left ribs, tightly and inextricably knotted to a similar string situated in the corresponding quarter of your little frame.

From *Jane Eyre* by Charlotte Brontë

I think . . . of so many men, so many minds, certainly so many hearts, so many kinds of love.

From *Anna Karenina* by Leo Tolstoy

How can I retrace today the strange steps of my obsession?

From *The Turn of the Screw* by Henry James

Much have we loved you. But speechless was our love, and with veils has it been veiled.

Yet now it cries aloud unto you, and would stand revealed before you.

And ever has it been that love knows not its own depth until the hour of separation.

From *The Prophet* by Khalil Gibran

After him I love
More than I love these eyes, more than my life,
More, by all mores, than e'er I shall love wife.
If I do feign, you witnesses above
Punish my life for tainting of my love.

From *Twelfth Night* by William Shakespeare

The silence, with which she listened to a proposal, dictated by love and despair, and enforced at a moment, when it seemed scarcely possible for her to oppose it;—when her heart was softened by the sorrows of a separation, that might be eternal, and her reason obscured by the illusions of love and terror, encouraged him to hope, that it would not be rejected.

From *The Mysteries of Udolpho* by Ann Radcliffe

Had I been in love, I could not have been more wretchedly blind. But vanity, not love, has been my folly.

From *Pride and Prejudice* by Jane Austen

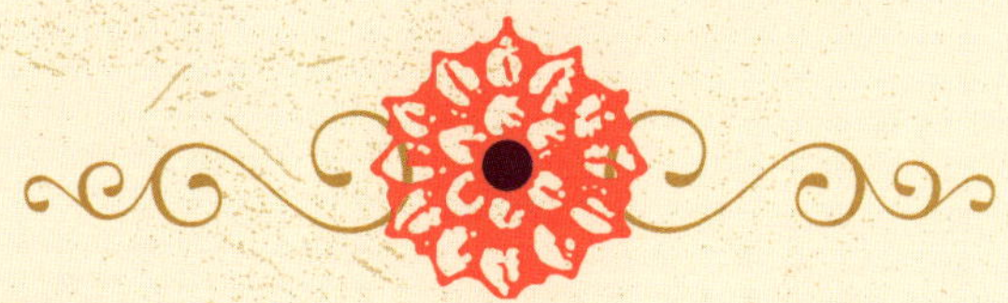

Raoul suffered, for she was very beautiful and he was shy and dared not confess his love, even to himself.

From *The Phantom of the Opera* by Gaston Leroux

. . . his honest heart would feel so much.

From *Northanger Abbey* by Jane Austen

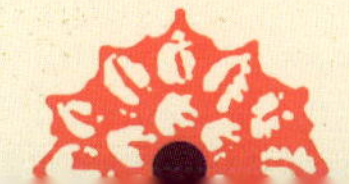

Their strong passions must either bruise or bend. They either slay the man, or themselves die. Shallow sorrows and shallow loves live on. The loves and sorrows that are great are destroyed by their own plenitude.

From *The Picture of Dorian Gray* by Oscar Wilde

. . . a beauty neither of fine color nor long eyelash, nor penciled brow, but of meaning, of movement, of radiance. Then her soul sat on her lips, and language flowed, from what source I cannot tell.

From *Jane Eyre* by Charlotte Brontë

I felt emotions of gentleness and pleasure, that had long appeared dead, revive within me. Half surprised by the novelty of these sensations, I allowed myself to be borne away by them, and forgetting my solitude and deformity, dared to be happy.

From *Frankenstein* by Mary Shelley

Sometimes after an hour of apathy, my strange and beautiful companion would take my hand and hold it with a fond pressure, renewed again and again; blushing softly, gazing in my face with languid and burning eyes, and breathing so fast that her dress rose and fell with the tumultuous respiration. It was like the ardor of a lover . . . and with gloating eyes she drew me to her, and her hot lips traveled along my cheek in kisses; and she would whisper, almost in sobs, "You are mine, you shall be mine, you and I are one forever."

From *Carmilla* by J. Sheridan Le Fanu

HOPE
DARKN

When lost in the depths of despair, nothing lights the way more than a beacon of love. Hope guides through somber grief and can break the chains of lasting melancholy. Only a spark is needed to ignite the light, and once burning it can catch into a blaze.

If I can stop one heart from breaking,
I shall not live in vain;
If I can ease one life the aching,
Or cool one pain,
Or help one fainting robin
Unto his nest again,
I shall not live in vain.

"If I Can Stop One Heart from Breaking"
by Emily Dickinson

If music be the food of love, play on,
Give me excess of it; that, surfeiting,
The appetite may sicken and so die.

From *Twelfth Night* by William Shakespeare

I ask one thing only: I ask for the right to hope, to suffer as I do. But if even that cannot be, command me to disappear, and I disappear. You shall not see me if my presence is distasteful to you.

From *Anna Karenina* by Leo Tolstoy

[When] suffering has been stronger than all other teaching, and has taught me to understand what your heart used to be. I have been bent and broken, but—I hope—into a better shape.

From *Great Expectations* by Charles Dickens

When poverty creeps in at the door, love flies in through the window. Our proverbs want rewriting. They were made in winter, and it is summer now; springtime for me, I think, a very dance of blossoms in blue skies.

From *The Picture of Dorian Gray* by Oscar Wilde

It is sinful to cherish those whom heaven has doomed to destruction.

From *Castle of Otranto* by Horace Walpole

Even in the grave, all is not lost.

From "The Pit and the Pendulum" by Edgar Allan Poe

Some of you say, "Joy is greater than sorrow," and others say, "Nay, sorrow is the greater."

But I say unto you, they are inseparable.

Together they come, and when one sits alone with you at your board, remember that the other is asleep upon your bed.

From *The Prophet* by Khalil Gibran

I've dreamt in my life dreams that have stayed with me ever after, and changed my ideas: they've gone through and through me, like wine through water, and altered the color of my mind.

From *Wuthering Heights* by Emily Brontë

JONATHAN HARKER AND MINA MURRAY

Life is full of challenges that can put even the strongest of relationships to the test. Financial stress, demanding careers, and children. Loss, grief, and health struggles. Vampires.

Jonathan Harker and his fiancée Mina Murray from Bram Stoker's *Dracula* suffer many of these troubles when Jonathan travels to Transylvania to assist the enigmatic Count Dracula in moving to London. Upon arriving at a dark and desolate castle, populated only by Dracula himself, three mysterious women, and a labyrinth of locked doors and windows, Jonathan quickly finds himself at the Count's mercy. Meanwhile in England, Mina worries for Jonathan, but is relieved to finally hear of his arrival at a Budapest hospital, where she immediately travels to help nurse her beloved back to health.

Once reunited, Jonathan and Mina take solace in each other's company and form a united front to face the threat of Dracula, who, having now arrived in London, is making every day a living nightmare. They act as each other's source of strength as Jonathan continues to suffer the repercussions of his time trapped by Dracula and as Mina is attacked by the Count and afflicted with the beginnings of vampirism herself. The couple relies on each other to defeat their fanged foe, with Mina's mystical connection to Dracula allowing them to track him and Jonathan's determination to free his now wife from vampirism fueling them. Mina and Jonathan show us that devotion to one another, love, and willful hope can help lead us out of even the darkest times and troubles, vampiric or otherwise.

O Rose thou art sick.
The invisible worm,
That flies in the night
In the howling storm:

Has found out thy bed
Of crimson joy:
And his dark secret love
Does thy life destroy.

"The Sick Rose" by William Blake

Thou wouldst be loved?—then let thy heart
From its present pathway part not!
Being everything which now thou art,
Be nothing which thou art not.
So with the world thy gentle ways,
Thy grace, thy more than beauty,
Shall be an endless theme of praise.
And love a simple duty.

"To Frances S. Osgood" by Edgar Allan Poe

They call you heartless: but your heart is true, and I love the bashfulness of your goodwill.

From *Thus Spake Zarathustra* by Friedrich Nietzsche

Our pleasures in this world are always to be paid for, and that we often purchase them at a great disadvantage, giving ready-monied actual happiness for a draft on the future, that may not be honored.

From *Northanger Abbey* by Jane Austen

No one but a woman can help a man when he is in trouble of the heart; and he had no one to comfort him.

From *Dracula* by Bram Stoker

You had brought me something higher,
something of which all art is but a reflection.
You had made me understand what love really
is. My love! My love! Prince Charming!
Prince of life! I have grown sick of shadows.
You are more to me than all art can ever be.

From *The Picture of Dorian Gray* by Oscar Wilde

Love is fearless in the midst of the sea of fear.

From "The Religion of Love" by Rumi

You are part of my existence, part of myself. You have been in every line I have ever read since I first came here, the rough common boy whose poor heart you wounded even then. You have been in every prospect I have ever seen since . . . You have been the embodiment of every graceful fancy that my mind has ever become acquainted with. The stones of which the strongest London buildings are made are not more real, or more impossible to be displaced by your hands, than your presence and influence have been to me, there and everywhere, and will be.

From *Great Expectations* by Charles Dickens

JANE EYRE AND EDWARD ROCHESTER

Jane Eyre and Mr. Rochester from Charlotte Brontë's 1847 *Jane Eyre* epitomize the classical gothic couple. Jane Eyre is hired as the governess of a young French girl named Adèle at Thornfield Hall, a beautiful but gloomy manor house owned by Mr. Edward Fairfax Rochester. She first meets Mr. Rochester after he is thrown off his horse and, despite his brusqueness, is assisted by Jane. Mr. Rochester's moods are unpredictable, and he possesses an air of mystery that perturbs even the levelheaded Jane. However, once establishing her wit and no-nonsense attitude, Mr. Rochester treats Jane as his equal and the two grow close. However, Mr. Rochester himself isn't the only mystery at Thornfield Hall; strange, almost supernatural occurrences plague the manor.

Despite the creepy happenings, Jane and Mr. Rochester grow ever closer. The two finally declare their love for each other, but during their wedding ceremony it is revealed that Mr. Rochester is already married to a mentally unwell woman who is the source of the mysterious occurrences. Despite her love for Mr. Rochester, Jane refuses to sacrifice her convictions and flees from Thornfield Hall. However, after some time, Jane hears the supernatural call of Mr. Rochester's voice and travels back to the now burned and desolate Thornfield Hall. Mr. Rochester, now a widower, sustained significant injuries in the fire, but Jane is simply overjoyed to be reunited with him as the two are finally free to happily spend the rest of their lives together in spite of their previous hardships.

They haven't an idea of what happiness is; they don't know that without our love, for us there is neither happiness nor unhappiness—no life at all.

From *Anna Karenina* by Leo Tolstoy

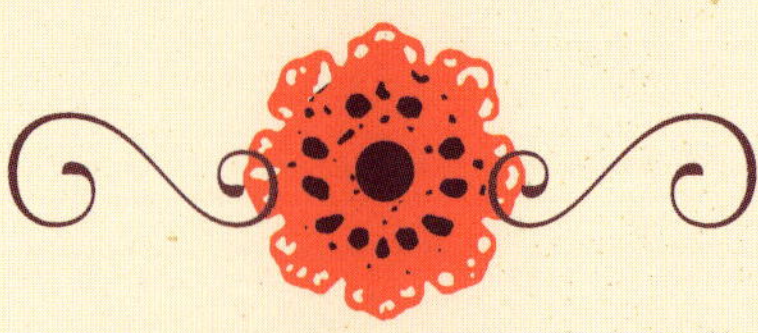

This—this is wicked. It would not be wicked to love me.

From *Jane Eyre* by Charlotte Brontë

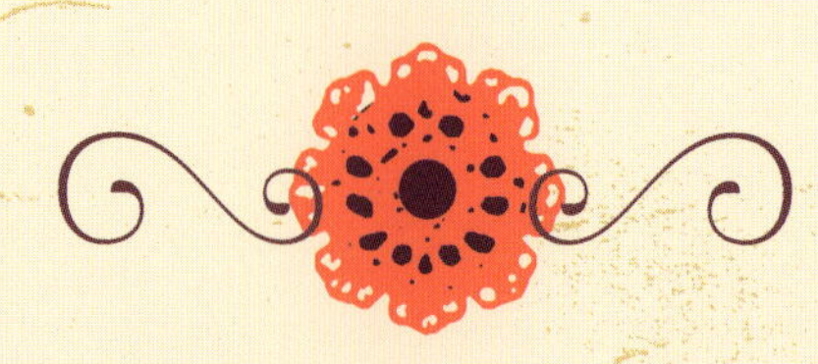

How mutable are our feelings, and how strange is that clinging love we have of life even in the excess of misery!

From *Frankenstein* by Mary Shelley

Ill suits it now the joys of love to know,
Too deep my anguish, and too wild my woe.

From *The Iliad* by Homer

I was there to protect and defend the little creatures in the world the most bereaved and the most lovable, the appeal of whose helplessness had suddenly become only too explicit, a deep, constant ache of one's own committed heart. We were cut off, really, together; we were united in our danger.

From *The Turn of the Screw* by Henry James

Go, brave heart, and save me from despair.

From *Little Women* by Louisa May Alcott

He put it very nicely, saying that he did not
want to wring my confidence from me,
but only to know, because if a woman's heart
was free a man might have hope.

From *Dracula* by Bram Stoker

All I wanted was to be loved for myself.

From *The Phantom of the Opera* by Gaston Leroux

Love those that hate you, but to love those one hates is impossible.

From *Anna Karenina* by Leo Tolstoy

. . . but still I loved life. This ridiculous foible is perhaps one of our most fatal characteristics; for is there anything more absurd than to wish to carry continually a burden which one can always throw down? To detest existence and yet to cling to one's existence? In brief, to caress the serpent which devours us, till he has eaten our very heart?

From *Candide* by Voltaire

HEART AND

The poignant beauty of lost love is a transformative experience. A heart opened to the majesty of love is just as susceptible to the agony of separation. An end to an epic love can feel like the end of the world, but new growth almost always buds from the ashes.

BREAK

You have killed my love. You used to stir my imagination. Now you don't even stir my curiosity. You simply produce no effect. I loved you because you were marvelous, because you had genius and intellect, because you realized the dreams of great poets and gave shape and substance to the shadows of art. You have thrown it all away.

From *The Picture of Dorian Gray* by Oscar Wilde

I met his kiss and I had to make, while
I folded him for a minute in my arms,
the most stupendous effort not to cry.

From *The Turn of the Screw* by Henry James

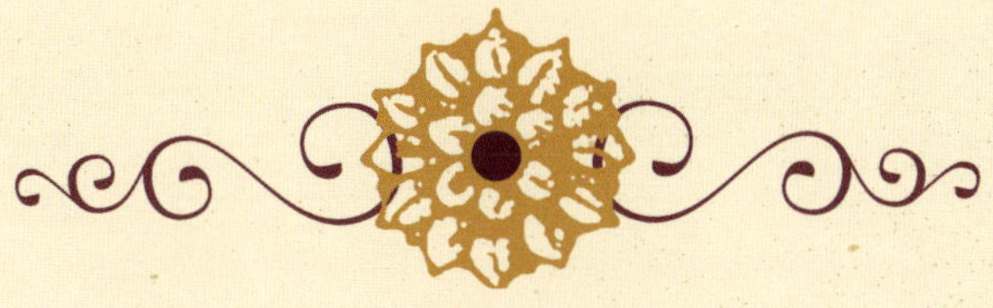

I have found a man who, before his spirit
had been broken by misery, I should have been
happy to have possessed as the brother
of my heart.

From *Frankenstein* by Mary Shelley

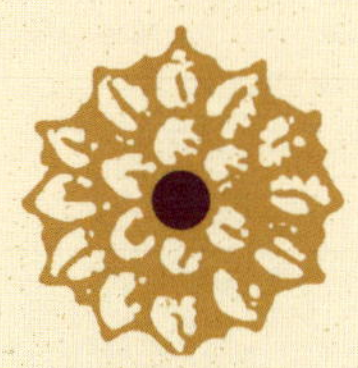

Heart, we will forget him!
You and I, tonight!
You may forget the warmth he gave,
I will forget the light.

When you have done, pray tell me,
That I my thoughts may dim;
Haste! lest while you're lagging,
I may remember him!

"Heart, We Will Forget Him" by Emily Dickinson

How can you, who long for the love and sympathy of man, persevere in this exile? You will return, and again seek their kindness, and you will meet with their detestation; your evil passions will be renewed, and you will then have a companion to aid you in the task of destruction.

From *Frankenstein* by Mary Shelley

"I wish I could love," cried Dorian Gray with a deep note of pathos in his voice. "But I seem to have lost the passion and forgotten the desire. I am too much concentrated on myself. My own personality has become a burden to me. I want to escape, to go away, to forget. It was silly of me to come down here at all . . . "

From *The Picture of Dorian Gray* by Oscar Wilde

My heart was fashioned to be susceptible of love and sympathy, and when wrenched by misery to vice and hatred, it did not endure the violence of the change without torture such as you cannot even imagine.

From *Frankenstein* by Mary Shelley

Bleeding hearts, and dry bones of the churchyard, and tears that burn as they fall—all dance together to the music that he make with that smileless mouth of him.

From *Dracula* by Bram Stoker

How the fond words, impassioned music low,
Sustain the sigh of love's divine regret.
No length of time may bid the heart forget.

From "Ode to Atthis" by Sappho

But you should not say the greatest romance of your life. You should say the first romance of your life. You will always be loved, and you will always be in love with love. A grand passion is the privilege of people who have nothing to do. That is the one use of the idle classes of a country. Don't be afraid. There are exquisite things in store for you. This is merely the beginning.

From *The Picture of Dorian Gray* by Oscar Wilde

For a long while now he hasn't loved me. And where love ends, hate begins.

From *Anna Karenina* by Leo Tolstoy

Dearest, your little heart is wounded; think me not cruel because I obey the irresistible law of my strength and weakness; if your dear heart is wounded, my wild heart bleeds with yours.

From *Carmilla* by J. Sheridan Le Fanu

To him alone her heart turned, and for him alone fell her bitter tears.

From *The Mysteries of Udolpho* by Ann Radcliffe

And that a young woman in love always looks—
"like Patience on a monument
"Smiling at Grief."

From *Northanger Abbey* by Jane Austen

If I returned, it was to be sacrificed or to see those whom I most loved die under the grasp of a demon whom I had myself created. I walked about the isle like a restless specter, separated from all it loved and miserable in the separation.

From *Frankenstein* by Mary Shelley

Break their hearts my pride and hope, break their hearts and have no mercy!

From *Great Expectations* by Charles Dickens

Those who are faithful know only the trivial side of love: it is the faithless who know love's tragedies.

From *The Picture of Dorian Gray* by Oscar Wilde

Because misery and degradation, and death, and nothing that God or Satan could inflict would have parted us, you, of your own will, did it. I have not broken your heart—you have broken it; and in breaking it, you have broken mine. So much the worse for me that I am strong. Do I want to live? What kind of living will it be when you—oh, God! Would you like to live with your soul in the grave?

From *Wuthering Heights* by Emily Brontë

ROMEO

Under love's heavy burden do I sink.

MERCUTIO

And, to sink in it, should you burden love—
Too great oppression for a tender thing.

ROMEO

Is love a tender thing? It is too rough,
Too rude, too boisterous, and it pricks like thorn.

MERCUTIO

If love be rough with you, be rough with love.
Prick love for pricking, and you beat love down.

From *Romeo and Juliet* by William Shakespeare

You don't know what you were to me, once.
Why, once . . . Oh, I can't bear to think of it!
I wish I had never laid eyes upon you! You
have spoiled the romance of my life. How little
you can know of love, if you say it mars your
art! Without your art, you are nothing . . .
The world would have worshiped you,
and you would have borne my name.

From *The Picture of Dorian Gray* by Oscar Wilde

You are miserable, are you not? Lonely, like
the devil, and envious like him? Nobody loves
you—nobody will cry for you when you die!
I wouldn't be you!

From *Wuthering Heights* by Emily Brontë

I LOVE YOU
LIKE A LIMB
THAT I COULD LIVE
WITHOUT,
BUT TO DO SO
WOULD BE
AGONIZING

Unknown Author

I know this love, that sovereign of hearts, that soul of our souls; yet it never cost me more than a kiss and twenty kicks on the backside. How could this beautiful cause produce in you an effect so abominable?

From *Candide* by Voltaire

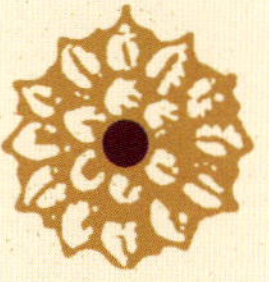

When one is in love, one always begins by deceiving one's self, and one always ends by deceiving others. That is what the world calls a romance.

From *The Picture of Dorian Gray* by Oscar Wilde

Nothing could be more charming than the way you take it, for of course if we're alone together now it's you that are alone most.

From *The Turn of the Screw* by Henry James

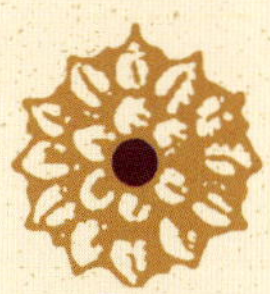

Even broken in spirit as he is, no one can feel more deeply than he does the beauties of nature. The starry sky, the sea, and every sight afforded by these wonderful regions seem still to have the power of elevating his soul from earth. Such a man has a double existence: he may suffer misery and be overwhelmed by disappointments, yet when he has retired into himself, he will be like a celestial spirit that has a halo around him, within whose circle no grief or folly ventures.

From *Frankenstein* by Mary Shelley

I am sick of women who love one. Women who hate one are much more interesting. Besides, the stuff is better.

From *The Picture of Dorian Gray* by Oscar Wilde

She loved me until all her love turned to poisonous hate when she knew that I thought more of my wife's footmark in the mud than I did of her whole body and soul.

From *The Memoirs of Sherlock Holmes* by Sir Arthur Conan Doyle

I gave him my heart, and he took and pinched it to death, and flung it back to me. People feel with their hearts, and since he has destroyed mine, I have not power to feel for him.

From *Wuthering Heights* by Emily Brontë

A frightful selfishness hurried me on, while my heart was poisoned with remorse.

From *Frankenstein* by Mary Shelley

Do you believe your heart to be, indeed, so hardened, that you can look without emotion on the suffering, to which you would condemn me?

From *The Mysteries of Udolpho* by Ann Radcliffe

ERIC DRAVEN
AND
SHELLY WEBSTER

Have you ever loved someone so much that you would come back to life for them? *The Crow*'s Eric Draven proved that he did when his fiancée Shelly Webster was brutally killed by a gang and he lost his life trying to protect her. His devotion didn't end there, as his love for Shelly and righteous anger at those who took her life caused a mystical crow to raise him from the dead to take revenge. Eric cloaks himself in black and leather, paints his face white with dark lips and eyes, and takes to the streets to avenge his and Shelly's deaths.

Even though Eric is physically invulnerable, the anguish of losing Shelly plagues him as reminders of their time together—their ruined apartment turned hideout, Shelly's engagement ring, and Sarah, the young girl who Eric and Shelly looked after—seem to follow him everywhere. While Eric spends most of his time paying back his and Shelly's suffering tenfold to their murderers, he honors Shelly's unmatched kindness in other ways. He comforts and protects Sarah and visits the dedicated police officer who stayed by Shelly's side during her final moments. Eric's every action is dedicated to avenging Shelly and protecting those who carry on her memory, and only when he finally rids the world of those who wronged them does his body begin to decay and his immortality begin to wane. As Eric kneels in front of their graves, Shelly, bathed in angelic light, comes to escort him to their final resting place, reuniting them in love and death.

SELECT WORKS CITED

Titles in bold indicate works of gothic literature.

Alcott, Louisa May. 1868. *Little Women.* Boston: Little, Brown, and Company.

Alighieri, Dante. 1885. *The Divine Comedy.* Translated by Rev. H. F. Cary, London: Cassell & Company, Limited.

Austen, Jane. 1803. *Northanger Abbey.* London: John Murray.

Austen, Jane. 1813. *Pride and Prejudice.* London: George Allen Publishers.

Brontë, Charlotte. 1897. *Jane Eyre.* London: Service & Paton.

Brontë, Emily. 1847. *Wuthering Heights.* London: Thomas Cautley Newby.

Browning, Elizabeth Barrett. 1906. *Sonnets from the Portuguese.* London: The Caradoc Press.

Byron, George Gordon, Lord. 1900. *The Works of Lord Byron: A New, Revised and Enlarged Edition, with Illustrations. Poetry. Vol. III.* London: Charles Scribner's Sons.

Dickens, Charles. 1867. *Great Expectations.* London: Chapman and Hall.

Dickinson, Emily. 1890. *Poems by Emily Dickinson, Three Series, Complete.* Edited by Mabel Loomis Todd and T. W. Higginson. Boston: Roberts Brothers.

Doyle, Sir Arthur Conan. 1890. "A Physiologist's Wife." *Blackwood Magazine.*

Doyle, Sir Arthur Conan. 1893. *The Memoirs of Sherlock Holmes.* London: G. Newnes Ltd.

Doyle, Sir Arthur Conan. 1895. *The Stark Munro Letters.* London: Longmans, Green & Co.

Doyle, Sir Arthur Conan. 1891. *The White Company. The Cornhill Magazine.*

Emerson, Ralph Waldo. 1904. *Poems: Household Edition.* Boston: Houghton, Mifflin and Company.

Fanu, Joseph Sheridan Le. 1871-1873. "Carmilla." *The Dark Blue.*

Fitzgerald, F. Scott. 1920. *This Side of Paradise.* New York: Charles Scribner's Sons.

Fitzgerald, F. Scott. 1925. *The Great Gatsby.* New York: Charles Scribner's Sons.

Gibran, Khalil. 1923. *The Prophet.* New York: Alfred A. Knopf.

Homer. 1899. *The Iliad.* Translated by Alexander Pope. London: Flaxman's Designs.

Hawthorne, Nathaniel. 1850. *The Scarlet Letter.* Boston: Ticknor, Reeds and Fields.

Henry VIII and Anne Boleyn. 1906. *The Love Letters of Henry VIII to Anne Boleyn.* Boston: D. B. Updike, The Merrymount Press.

James, Henry. 1898. *The Turn of the Screw.* New York City: Macmillan.

Leroux, Gaston. 1911. *The Phantom of the Opera.* New York: The Bobb-Merrill Company Publishers.

Maugham, W. Somerset. 1915. *On Human Bondage.* New York: George H. Durran and Company.

Montgomery, L. M. 1909. *Anne of Avonlea.* Boston: L. C. Page & Company.

Nietzche, Friederich. 1896. *Thus Spake Zarathustra.* Translated by Thomas Common. London: H. Henry & Co.

O'Hara, John Myers. 1907. *The Poems of Sappho.* Portland: Smith & Sale, Publishers.

Poe, Edgar Allan. 1888. *The Complete Poetical Works of Edgar Allan Poe.* Edited by John H. Ingram. London and New York: Frederick Warne & Co.

Poe, Edgar Allan. 1883. *The Works of Edgar Allan Poe: The Raven Edition.* Edinburgh: A. & C. Black.

Radcliffe, Ann. 1794. *The Mysteries of Udolpho.* London: G. G. and J. Robinson.

Rossetti, Christina Georgina. 1906. *Poems.* Boston: Little, Brown, and Company.

Rumi. 1881. *Mesnevi.* Translated by James W. Redhouse. London: Trübner & Co., Ludgate Hill.

Rumi. 1920. *The Persian Mystics.* London: John Murray, Albemarle Street, W.

Shakespeare, William. 1597. *Romeo and Juliet.* London: John Danter and Edward Allde.

Shakespeare, William. 1623. *Twelfth Night (or What You Will).* London: First Folio.

Shelley, Mary. 1818. *Frankenstein.* London: Henry Colburn and Richard Bentley.

Shelley, Percy Bysshe. 1914. *The Complete Poetical Works of Percy Bysshe Shelley Volume 2.* Edited by Thomas Hutchinson. Oxford: The Oxford Wordsworth.

Stacpool, H. de Vere. 1863. *Sappho: A New Rendering.* London: Hutchinson and Co.

Stoker, Bram. 1897. *Dracula.*London: Archibald Constable and Company.

Tolstoy, Leo. 1886. *Anna Karenina.* New York: Crowell.

Voltaire. 1918. *Candide.* New York: Boni & Liverlight, Inc.

Walpole, Horace. 1764. *The Castle of Otranto.* London: Thomas Lownds.

Wilde, Oscar. 1899. *The Importance of Being Earnest.* London: Leonard Smithers and Co.

Wilde, Oscar. 1890. "The Picture of Dorian Gray." *Lippincot's Monthly Magazine.*

Wollstonecraft, Mary. 1908. *The Love Letters of Mary Wollstonecraft to Gilbert Imlay.* London: Hutchinson & Co.

Wordsworth, William. 1896. *The Poetical Works of William Wordsworth, Vol. II.* Edited by William Knight. London: Frederick Warne.

Yeats, William Butler. 1908. *Poems Lyrical and Narrative.* Stratford-on-Avon: Shakespeare Head Press.

FURTHER READING

Expand your gothic library with the following texts.

A Dowry of Blood by S. T. Gibson

Anatomy: A Love Story by Dana Schwartz

House of Hunger by Alexis Henderson

Jamaica Inn by Daphne du Maurier

Mexican Gothic by Silvia Moreno-Garcia

Rebecca by Daphne du Maurier

The Hacienda by Isabel Cañas

The King of the Castle by Victoria Holt

Compilation and Introduction © 2026 by
Quarto Publishing Group USA Inc.

First published in 2026 by Castle Books,
an imprint of The Quarto Group,
142 West 36th Street, 4th Floor,
New York, NY 10018, USA
(212) 779-4972
www.Quarto.com

EEA Representation, WTS Tax d.o.o.,
Žanova ulica 3, 4000 Kranj, Slovenia.
www.wts-tax.si

All rights reserved. No part of this book may be reproduced in any form without written permission of the copyright owners. All images included in this book are original works created by the artist credited on the copyright page, not generated by artificial intelligence, and have been reproduced with the knowledge and prior consent of the artist. The producer, publisher, and printer accept no responsibility for any infringement of copyright or otherwise arising from the contents of this publication. Every effort has been made to ensure that credits accurately comply with the information supplied. We apologize for any inaccuracies that may have occurred and will address inaccurate or missing information in a subsequent reprinting of the book

Castle titles are also available at discount for retail, wholesale, promotional, and bulk purchase. For details, contact the Special Sales Manager by email at specialsales@quarto.com or by mail at The Quarto Group, Attn: Special Sales Manager, 100 Cummings Center Suite 265D, Beverly, MA 01915 USA.

10 9 8 7 6 5 4 3 2 1

ISBN: 978-1-57715-567-6

Digital edition published in 2026
eISBN: 978-0-7603-9984-2

Group Publisher: Rage Kindelsperger
Creative Director: Laura Drew
Managing Editor: Cara Donaldson
Editorial Assistant: Chloe Gerhard
Cover and Interior Design:
Silvia Virgillo • puntuale

Printed in Huizhou, Guangdong, China
TT102025

This book provides general information on various widely known and widely accepted images that tend to evoke feelings of love and devotion. However, it should not be relied upon as recommending or promoting any specific diagnosis or method of treatment for a particular condition, and it is not intended as a substitute for medical or mental health advice or for direct diagnosis and treatment of a medical or mental health condition by a qualified physician. Readers who have questions about a particular condition, possible treatments for that condition, or possible reactions from the condition or its treatment should consult a physician or other qualified health care professional.

The Quarto Group denounces any and all forms of hate, discrimination, and oppression and does not condone the use of its products in any practices aimed at harming or demeaning any group or individual.